No More, Por Favor

Susan Middleton Elya pictures by David Walker

G. P. Putnam's Sons • An Imprint of Penguin Group (USA) Inc.

Glossary and Pronunciation Guide

aguacates (ah gwah KAH tehs) avocados

ay (EYE) oh my

bebé (beh BEH) baby

boca (BOE kah) mouth

cena (SEH nah) supper

colibrí (koe lee BREE) hummingbird

comida (koe MEE dah) food

día (DEE ah) day

diferente (dee feh REHN teh) different

en frente (EHN FREHN teh) in front

ensalada (ehn sah LAH dah) salad

fiesta (FYEHS tah) party

finito (fee NEE toe) finished (Italian)

granadas (grah NAH dahs) pomegranates

 guacamayo (gwah kah MAH yoe) macaw

hermosa (ehr MOE sah) beautiful

la (LAH) the (singular)

los quetzales (LOCE keht SAH lehs) the tropical bird family

madre (MAH dreh) mother

Mamá (mah MAH) Mom

 iguana

 mango

papaya

mariposa (mah ree POE sah) butterfly

mesa (MEH sah) table

mi vida (MEE VEE dah) my life

mono (MOE noe) monkey

monito (moe NEE toe) little monkey

nada (NAH dah) nothing

no es buena (NO EHS BWEH nah) it isn't good

no más (NOE MAHS) no more

oye (OE yeh) listen

toucan

Papá (pah PAH) Dad

papagayo (pah pah GAH yoe) parrot

para ti, para mí (pah rah TEE, pah rah MEE) for you, for me

piña (PEE nyah) pineapple

plátanos frescos (PLAH tah noce FREHS koce) fresh bananas

por favor (por fah VOHR) please

quetzalito (keht sah LEE toe) little quetzal, a tropical bird

selva (SEHL vah) rain forest

semillas (seh MEE yahs) seeds

sorpresa (sohr PREH sah) surprise

Deep in **la selva**, a tropical place,
lives **Mamá Mono**. Her son makes a face.

"I see bananas. Do you want to eat?
Plátanos frescos would make a good treat."

"No," says **Monito**. "They taste sort of funky."

"¡Ay!" says **Mamá**. "Such a finicky monkey."

Deep in the rain forest–**selva**, so green,
lives **Papagayo**, an eating machine.

"Here, **Bebé** Parrot, papaya is yummy."
"No!" says the baby. "No more in my tummy!

Papaya for breakfast, for lunch and **la cena**.
Too many times in a row **no es buena**!"

Deep in the rain forest–**selva**, so wild,
lives **Mamá** Toucan with one picky child.

Pomegranate seeds have left ruby stains.

"**Granadas** are messy!" her baby complains.

"Too many seeds! **Semillas** unending!

These are not tasty, and I'm done pretending."

Deep in the rain forest–**selva**, so lush,
lives Ms. Iguana, whispering, "Hush!"

Baby is whining and does the spoon tango.

Mom tries to feed him. He wants no more mango.

He clamps shut his **boca**, refuses to eat.

"**Oye**, **Mamá**, this fruit is too sweet."

Deep in the rain forest, Dad **Mariposa**
drinks all he can from a petal **hermosa**.

"Here, Little Butterfly, have a big sip."
"Not one more slurp or I think I might flip!

Three times each **día**, it's always the same.
Please, not that flower, **Papá**. It's so lame!"

Deep in **la selva**, layered with life,
live **los Quetzales**: a kid, dad and wife.

They love avocados, except **Quetzalito**.
"No **aguacates**! I'm done now–*finito*!

The fruit is too squishy and squashy and green.
Since yesterday morning, I've eaten thirteen!"

Deep in the rain forest–**selva**, so busy,
lives **Colibrí**, with her son in a tizzy.

"Syrupy goo–I'm sick of the smell.
I'm tired of nectar to drink. Can't you tell?

Flowers–**no más**!" He flits there **en frente**.

"Hummingbird kids need food **diferente**!"

Deep in **la selva**, steaming with mist,
lives a macaw and the chick she just kissed.

Asks **Guacamayo**, "Pineapple chunk?"
"I don't want **piña!**" The chick makes it thunk.

"It's too tart and stringy," he says as it bounces.
"You squirted my eyeball," his **madre** announces.

She blinks out the juice, then has a good thought.
*Will I serve him **piña** again? I think NOT!*

Deep in the jungle, a midweek **sorpresa**.
Kids all arrive at a rain forest **mesa**.

"Why are we here?" asks Hummingbird Baby.
"Is it a **fiesta** or playgroup day?" Maybe.

"Look at the table, filled with **comida**!
It's the most food that I've seen in **mi vida**!"

What's that new smell? This texture? That blossom?
Everyone has the same thought. This is awesome!

Piñas are eaten by small **Papagayo**.
Mangos are tasted by young **Guacamayo**.

Two nectar kids–**Mariposa**, **Colibrí**,
trade types of blooms. **"¡Para ti, para mí!"**

Bananas, avocados, **granadas** to share.
"How many seeds can you spit?" babies dare.

Sounds of contentment—they squawk, warble, chirp.
They laugh when **Monito** lets out a big burp.

BURRRP!

A nice change of pace is their fruit **ensalada**.
And what could be better than sharing it? **¡Nada!**

To Teresa and her two grown babies, Alex and Rachael. –S.M.E.

For our silly, wiggly, giggly Sofia. –D.W.

G. P. PUTNAM'S SONS • A division of Penguin Young Readers Group.
Published by The Penguin Group.
Penguin Group (USA) Inc., 375 Hudson Street, New York, NY 10014, U.S.A.
Penguin Group (Canada), 90 Eglinton Avenue East, Suite 700, Toronto, Ontario M4P 2Y3, Canada (a division of Pearson Penguin Canada Inc.).
Penguin Books Ltd, 80 Strand, London WC2R 0RL, England.
Penguin Ireland, 25 St. Stephen's Green, Dublin 2, Ireland (a division of Penguin Books Ltd.).
Penguin Group (Australia), 250 Camberwell Road, Camberwell, Victoria 3124, Australia (a division of Pearson Australia Group Pty Ltd).
Penguin Books India Pvt Ltd, 11 Community Centre, Panchsheel Park, New Delhi - 110 017, India.
Penguin Group (NZ), 67 Apollo Drive, Rosedale, North Shore 0632, New Zealand (a division of Pearson New Zealand Ltd).
Penguin Books (South Africa) (Pty) Ltd, 24 Sturdee Avenue, Rosebank, Johannesburg 2196, South Africa.
Penguin Books Ltd, Registered Offices: 80 Strand, London WC2R 0RL, England.

Published simultaneously in Canada. Manufactured in China by South China Printing Co. Ltd.
Design by Katrina Damkoehler. Text set in Cafeteria. The art was done with layers of acrylic paint on paper.

Library of Congress Cataloging-in-Publication Data
Elya, Susan Middleton, 1955-
No more, por favor / Susan Middleton Elya ; pictures by David Walker.   p. cm.
Summary: Rain forest parents come up with a solution when all their children become picky eaters at the same time.
Spanish words interspersed in the rhyming text are defined in a glossary.
[1. Stories in rhyme. 2. Rain forest animals–Fiction. 3. Food habits–Fiction. 4. Parent and child–Fiction.] I. Walker, David, 1965- ill. II. Title.
PZ8.3.E514No 2010   [E]–dc22   2008048411
ISBN 978-0-399-24766-8

1 3 5 7 9 10 8 6 4 2